DISNEY · PIXAR

THE INCREDIBLES

∿ **BOOK FIVE** ∿

DISNEP PRESS

New York • Los Angeles

Mr. Incredible was a Super—a hero with special powers. His greatest fan was a boy named Buddy. Buddy wanted to be a Super, too. He invented rocket boots that allowed him to fly. He even asked Mr. Incredible if he could be his sidekick. But Mr. Incredible told Buddy that fancy boots didn't make someone a Super. Supers were born, not made.

Mr. Incredible married a Super named Elastigirl. She could stretch into any shape.

One day, Mr. Incredible saved someone who did not want to be saved. Mr. Incredible was sued. Soon, lots of people were suing Supers. The government told the Supers not to use their powers anymore. They had to go into hiding and live like normal people in the Super Relocation Program.

Mr. Incredible and Elastigirl became Bob and Helen Parr. They lived in the suburbs and had three kids—Violet, Dash, and Jack-Jack. They tried their best to be normal, but it was difficult. Violet could generate force fields and turn invisible. Dash had Super speed. Only little Jack-Jack didn't seem to have any powers.

Bob missed saving people. So did his friend Lucius. He had once been a Super named Frozone. One night, Bob and Lucius saved some people from a fire. The next day, a woman named Mirage contacted Bob. She knew he was a Super and offered him a secret mission.

Bob knew this was his chance to make a difference. He told Helen he had a business trip and then got on a plane with Mirage.

The two flew to a secret island. Mirage told Bob that the government had lost control of a robot called the Omnidroid.

"Every moment you spend fighting it only increases its knowledge of how to beat you," Mirage said.

Mr. Incredible used all of his strength against the Omnidroid. At last, he tricked it into defeating itself.

When Mr. Incredible went home, he felt like a new man. He even had his friend Edna Mode design a new Super suit for him.

Soon, Mirage contacted Mr. Incredible again. She had another mission for him. But when Mr. Incredible arrived, he learned that Mirage was not all she seemed. Her boss was Buddy, the boy who had wanted to be Mr. Incredible's sidekick. He was all grown up and went by the name Syndrome.

Syndrome had invented the Omnidroid to make himself more powerful. He tried to capture Mr. Incredible, but the Super escaped.

In an underwater cave, Mr. Incredible found the remains of Gazerbeam, a Super who had died battling the Omnidroid. Mr. Incredible knew he had to stop Buddy!

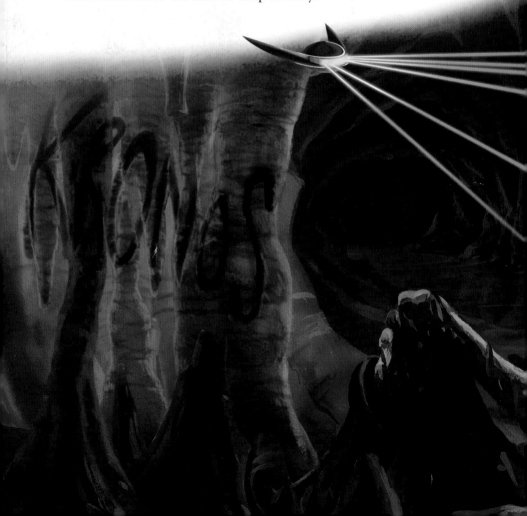

Back at home, Helen began to suspect that Bob was up to something. She went to visit Edna Mode.

Edna was thrilled to see Helen. She'd had so much fun making Bob's new suit that she'd made one for Helen, too. In fact, she had made new suits for the whole family! Each suit came with a homing device for handy tracking.

Helen put on her Super suit and activated Bob's homing device. As she flew toward the homing signal, she discovered that Dash and Violet had stowed away with her.

Just then, a missile hit the plane they were flying on. The plane went down and landed in the ocean. Elastigirl shaped herself into a boat, and Dash used his Super speed to power them toward the island where Bob was in trouble.

Back on the island, Syndrome had captured Mr. Incredible. From his prison cell, Mr. Incredible listened to the attack on his family.

Desperate, Mr. Incredible grabbed Mirage. "Release me now, or I'll crush her," he said.

But Syndrome did not care. He knew that Mr. Incredible would never hurt anyone, no matter how upset he was.

Meanwhile, Mr. Incredible's family arrived on the island.
Elastigirl brought the children to a cave. She told them to stay
put and then left to find their father.

Suddenly, a huge ball of fire filled the cave. Dash and Violet
fled. The fire was the rocket exhaust from Syndrome's base. He
had launched his Omnidroid toward the city.

Elastigirl found her husband inside Syndrome's
headquarters. Mirage was angry that Syndrome had been
willing to let Mr. Incredible hurt her. Realizing how evil
Syndrome was, she let Mr. Incredible go.

Mr. Incredible and Elastigirl raced to Violet and Dash,
who had been surrounded by Syndrome's guards. Together,
the family fought off the henchmen.

Just then, Syndrome arrived. He used an immobi-ray to freeze the Supers. Then he flew off to the city, where his Omnidroid was already wreaking havoc. He planned to defeat the robot in front of the whole city. Then everyone would think he was a hero!

Violet used a force field to break the immobi-ray's hold on her. She freed the rest of her family, and they flew to the city.

When they arrived, the Omnidroid was destroying everything. Syndrome tried to use a remote control to stop it, but the robot had become too powerful. It knocked Syndrome out.

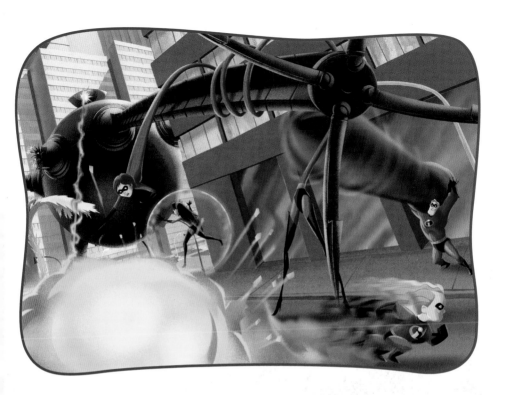

It was up to the Supers to save the day. Individually, they were awesome. As a team, they were unstoppable! Their old friend Frozone showed up, and together they defeated the Omnidroid.

The people of the city cheered, glad that the Supers had returned.

When the Incredibles got home, Syndrome was flying above their house with Jack-Jack. Suddenly, the baby turned into a little monster. The villain dropped him. As he fell, Jack-Jack pulled off part of Syndrome's rocket boot. The villain plummeted to the ground—gone forever.

Mr. Incredible threw Elastigirl into the air. She caught Jack-Jack and brought him safely back to the ground.